THE TERRACOTTA GIRL

A Story of Ancient China

by Jessica Gunderson

illustrated by Caroline Hu

PICTURE WINDOW BOOKS
Minneapolis, Minnesota

Editor: Shelly Lyons
Designer: Tracy Davies
Page Production: Michelle Biedscheid
Art Director: Nathan Gassman
Associate Managing Editor: Christianne Jones
The illustrations in this book were created with
brushed pen and ink.

Picture Window Books
151 Good Counsel Drive
P.O. Box 669
Mankato, MN 56002-0669
877-845-8392
www.picturewindowbooks.com

Printed in the United States of America.

All books published by Picture Window Books
are manufactured with paper containing at least
10 percent post-consumer waste.

Library of Congress Cataloging-in-Publication Data
Gunderson, Jessica.
The terracotta girl : a story of ancient China /
by Jessica Gunderson ; illustrated by Caroline Hu.
p. cm. — (Read-it! chapter books. Historical tales)
ISBN 978-1-4048-4737-8 (library binding)
1. China—History—Qin dynasty, 221-207 B.C.—
Juvenile fiction. [1. China—History—Qin dynasty, 221-
207 B.C.—Fiction. 2. Sex role—Fiction.] I. Hu, Caroline,
ill. II. Title.
PZ7.G963Te 2008
[Fic]—dc22   2008006309

TABLE OF CONTENTS

WORDS TO KNOW

Confucius—a Chinese philosopher whose teachings still influence many Asian citizens and others around the world

Great Wall of China—a 4,000-mile (6,400-kilometer) wall that stretches across northern China

mercury—a poisonous metal that is liquid at ordinary temperatures: the ancient Chinese believed mercury would help them live longer

Qin Dynasty (221 B.C.–A.D. 206)—the First Emperor of China, Qin Shi Huangdi, reigned during this period: in 221 B.C., the kingdoms of China were unified, forming one country

terracotta—a brownish-orange clay

tomb—a house, chamber, or vault for the dead

INTRODUCTION

210 B.C.—Qin Dynasty

Confucius, the wise scholar, said: "The brave are not afraid."

I will tell you a story unlike any you have ever heard. It is a story about bravery. It is a story about fear. It is the story of how I became the emperor's warrior.

It is easy to believe you are brave when you have no reason to be afraid. When I was young, I thought I was brave. I had never felt fear. I thought I would never be afraid of anything. In my mind, I was already a warrior.

To be a warrior, you must conquer your enemies. A true warrior, one that people will remember for centuries, is one who conquers even death.

I became that warrior.

But, you say, many warriors have conquered their enemies. Many warriors are brave. How is my story unlike any other?

I will tell you—you see, it is because I am a girl.

4

I lived during China's first years, during the dark days of Qin Shi Huangdi, First Emperor of China.

Many will tell you that the First Emperor was a good emperor. And he was. He created one single country out of many small ones. He named that country China. For that he will always be remembered.

Those who believe he was an evil emperor will never say it aloud. Even now that he is dead, no one dares to speak ill of him.

But I will tell you that he was harsh and sometimes cruel. He punished the innocent. He made us work like slaves to build his roads and his Great Wall.

He didn't want anyone, especially a little girl, telling him what to do.

I will come to that later. For now, I will
tell you that my father and I lived in a
hut in the country. My father worked in
the sun, wind, and rain, helping to build
the Great Wall of China.

"It takes hundreds of men to build one good country," my father used to say.

"And women," I muttered as I stirred rice for his supper, sewed his clothes, mended his shoes, and swept the floor.

My father only laughed.

I thought I lived a miserable life. All day I worked in the wheat fields. And when I came home, I took care of my father.

I watched with envy as the First Emperor's warriors passed. I was as brave as those boys. I wished to be a warrior like them. I longed for my life to change, though not in the way that it did.

One chilly dawn, a messenger arrived for my father. "Ran Jie-shu instructs you to go to Chang'an as fast as your legs can carry you," the messenger said.

My father clasped a hand over his heart. "Ran Jie-shu!" he exclaimed. "He is an old friend. I heard he was building the emperor's army. Oh, what great pleasure! What great joy! He wishes me to be a warrior."

I eyed my father doubtfully. He was an old man. How could he become a warrior?

That night, my father prepared for his journey. He packed his bag. I wished I could join him.

"Don't just stand there, Yung-lu," he scolded. "Fetch my mercury."

Every night, my father took mercury. Like many people at that time, he believed mercury would make him live forever.

"The emperor takes mercury pills, too," he often said proudly.

That night, he wanted to take two pills.

"No, Father," I said. "What if that's too much?"

But he took the pills anyway.

Although my father had believed the mercury would make him stronger, that night he grew very ill and died. I was filled with sadness. For the first time in my life, I was afraid. *What would I do? Where would I go?* I wondered.

I kept remembering the messenger's urgent message and my father's words. "Ran Jie-shu is building an army," my father had said. "He needs warriors."

I said goodbye to the wheat fields and our hut and set off for Chang'an.

CHAPTER TWO

The journey to Chang'an was long. I ate the rice I had brought along. When that was gone, I caught rabbits and mice and cooked them over a fire.

Many who passed called out to me. "Little girl, where are you going all alone?" they asked.

"My father is dead," I answered. "I'm going to become a warrior."

"Ha! You are a girl," they said. "You cannot be a warrior."

But I did not listen to them. I kept my head high and marched on with courage, though inside I was deeply afraid.

When I reached the city of Chang'an, I asked everyone where I could find Ran Jie-shu. No one knew.

"He is building an army for Emperor Qin," I said. "You must know him!"

But they shook their heads.

Finally, one man gave me the answer
I wished for. He lowered his voice and
said, "You will find the army near Mount
Lishan. But be careful. No one is to know
the army is there. Don't breathe a word."

I traveled toward Mount Lishan. I was hungry and tired. I saw children playing along the road. I wished I could join them.

But if I wanted to become a warrior, I could not give up.

I saw an old man resting near a tree. "Where can I find Ran Jie-shu?" I asked the man.

"Ran Jie-shu?" he repeated. "Why, that is me!"

I stared at him. He was old. He looked as though he could not walk without stumbling. How could this man be the leader of an army?

"I have made a mistake," I said.

I turned the horse back toward the road, but the man called out. "Tan Rui?" he asked.

I stopped and looked back. Tan Rui was my father's name.

"I am not—" I began to say.

"I asked for Tan Rui, and instead here is a little child," Ran Jie-shu said.

I looked at him angrily. Couldn't he see that I was not a child? I was a girl, a brave girl!

As I dismounted my horse, I said, "Tan Rui was my father. I am Yung-lu. I am here to become a warrior in his place."

Ran Jie-shu laughed and said, "No matter who your father was, you are still a *girl*."

I turned away. I did not want to give up. But he was right. Girls were not allowed to be warriors.

As I walked toward the road, I saw a grand sight in the distance. A large group of soldiers was marching toward me, carrying a throne on their shoulders. On the throne sat a man covered in jewels and silk. Emperor Qin!

I crouched behind a tree and stared as the royal group passed.

The emperor called out to his guards, "Guard! More tea! Fan me!"

Then he shouted, "Guard! Bring my mercury pills!"

Mercury! I thought. *That was what had killed my father.*

I leaped out from behind the tree and rushed toward Emperor Qin. "No!" I cried. "Mercury will kill you!"

You might wonder what made me think the emperor would listen. You might wonder why I would try to save such a harsh, selfish leader at all.

You see, my father had spent his life building the Great Wall for the emperor. I could not let the emperor die.

Emperor Qin halted his soldiers. He glared down at me. His eyes boiled with anger.

"What did you say?" he shouted.

"Mercury killed my father. It will kill you, too," I told him.

"No one tells Emperor Qin what to do. Get out of my sight!" he cried.

Maybe he will listen, I thought as I scurried back to the tree. *Maybe he won't take any more pills.*

But I doubted it.

"You're lucky," said a voice from behind me. "He might have thrown you in jail."

It was Ran Jie-shu.

I shook my head. "I don't feel lucky. I have no home, and I will never be a warrior."

Ran Jie-Shu nodded. "The emperor would be very angry to find a girl in his army," he said. "But the emperor is not a kind man. He does not deserve to have everything he wants!"

Ran Jie-shu took my arm. "Come with me," he said. "I have something important to show you."

CHAPTER THREE

I ran to keep up with Ran Jie-shu as he moved through the trees. For an old man, he was very quick.

He stopped in front of a great boulder. He listened. Then he pushed aside the rock and motioned for me to enter a cave.

27

The cave twisted and turned below the earth. I gulped. Fear spread through me. This place was very dark.

We walked down into the darkness. Finally, I saw candles burning along the cave walls. I breathed a sigh of relief as we entered a lit room. I stopped. My relief turned to fear.

I was face-to-face with hundreds of soldiers! Their weapons were perched at their sides. I screamed.

Ran Jie-shu laughed.

My scream bounced against the walls and echoed back to me. The soldiers did not move.

They were terracotta statues—hundreds of them. Each statue held a real weapon.

"This is the emperor's secret tomb,"
Ran Jie-shu said. "These are the warriors
who will guard him in the next world."

The tomb was no ordinary tomb.
It was an underground palace. Jewels
sparkled on the ceiling like stars. An
ivory throne stood at the front of the
tomb. But nothing was more amazing
than the terracotta army. I walked
through the rows of warriors. Each face
was different. They looked so real I
had to poke them to make sure they
weren't alive.

"I have sculpted many of these warriors," Ran Jie-shu told me. "You showed great bravery today. Would you like to become a warrior?"

As you might have guessed, this was not what I wanted. I had hoped to be a *real* warrior, to fight in a *real* war. But as I looked around at the terracotta army, I felt an urge to be one of them. I wanted the honor of guarding Emperor Qin forever.

"Yes," I replied. "I will be one of your warriors."

CHAPTER FOUR

Over the next few days, I stood very still while Ran Jie-shu studied my face. Then he sculpted from clay my face, arms, and body. I was amazed at how much the statue looked like me.

But I was worried, too. The statue was a girl soldier. What would the emperor do when he found out there was a *girl* in his army?

One day, a loud voice echoed through the tomb. "The emperor," Ran Jie-shu said. "Hide quickly!"

I gulped. If Emperor Qin saw me or my terracotta warrior, Ran Jie-shu and I were as good as dead. I crouched behind a statue. The massive silver shield it held guarded me from the emperor's gaze.

"The tomb will take many more years to be ready," Emperor Qin said to his guards. "It needs more jewels. More ivory. More soldiers!"

His booming voice echoed throughout the tomb.

"But it does not matter," Emperor Qin continued. "I will not need this tomb. I will live forever. Guards! Bring me my mercury pills at once."

Ran Jie-shu looked at me as though he knew what I was going to do.

I could not let the emperor die—not after everything my father had done in his service.

When the guard brought Emperor Qin the pills, I crept out from behind the statue. I hid in the shadows behind the emperor. As he lifted the pills to his mouth, I reached out and tugged his arm. The pills spilled to the ground.

I thought I could outrun the guards.
But I could not. They caught me and
carried me back to the emperor.

I was doomed.

"You again!" Emperor Qin spat. "I
warned you."

"And I warned you!" I said. "But you
will not listen."

36

"Hush!" he cried. "Guards, take the girl away. Kill her!"

As the guards grabbed my arms, Ran Jie-shu stepped from the shadows. He bowed low.

"Emperor Qin," he began, "please spare this girl. She is my helper. She is here only to serve you."

The emperor glared at Ran Jie-shu. A long moment passed, and then he said, "You are my finest sculptor. I will give her another chance. But you both must pay the price. You both will serve me for the rest of your lives. You will never leave this tomb!"

The guards dropped my arms. I ran to
Ran Jie-shu.

Emperor Qin turned to the guards and
demanded, "Seal the entrances so these
fools can never escape."

Then he turned and marched away.
His guards followed, leaving Ran Jie-shu
and me alone in the dark, silent tomb.

CHAPTER FIVE

"Don't worry, Yung-lu," Ran Jie-shu said cheerfully. "There are worse places to spend the rest of your life." He pulled a candle from his pocket and lit it.

I looked around at the jeweled walls
and ivory throne. Suddenly they did not
seem so splendid. "I guess," I said.

"Besides," Ran Jie-shu went on, "I
know a secret exit."

"You do?" I asked. "Then let's get out
of here!"

Ran Jie-shu shook his head. "No,"
he said. "Your warrior is unfinished. I
cannot leave."

41

No matter how much I begged,
Ran Jie-shu refused to leave until my
soldier was finished. She was the most
beautiful statue I had ever seen. She
stood noble among the other soldiers.

She looked brave, much braver than I felt.

I was proud to look at her. But I was embarrassed, too. Why did I deserve such an honor? All I had done was put Ran Jie-shu and myself in danger.

Finally, the statue was finished. I took a last look at her as Ran Jie-shu and I made our way toward the entrance. No matter how evil the emperor was, my terracotta girl would always serve him.

Suddenly, a crash broke the silence
of the tomb. We heard footsteps coming
toward us in the dim light. Someone else
was in the tomb! Ran Jie-shu quickly
blew out the candle.

I could see two shadowy figures
lurking ahead. I gripped Ran Jie-shu's
hand and crouched behind a group of
warrior statues. Squinting to get a better
look, I watched the figures move between
the rows of soldiers. They stopped near
each one.

Then I realized what they were doing. "Thieves," I whispered. "They are stealing from the emperor! We must stop them!"

You might wonder why I thought that I could stop them. You might think that I should have learned to keep quiet. I could not stop the emperor from taking mercury. How was I supposed to stop thieves from stealing?

But I did not think any of this. I leaped from behind the statue. "Stop!" I yelled.

The thieves looked up, surprised. I hadn't realized the thieves were stealing the weapons.

They charged at me, swords glinting in their hands. I stumbled backward, almost knocking over a terracotta soldier. A spear in the soldier's hand clattered to my feet.

I picked it up. It looked familiar. It looked like one I had seen many times.

I raised my eyes and looked at the
soldier's face. It was a statue of my father.
My father's spear, the spear I had always
wanted for myself, was now in my hands.
I whirled and let the spear fly. It quivered
in the air, then dived and knocked the
weapon from one thief's grip.

The sword landed on the other thief's foot. He howled in pain. It couldn't have been more perfect.

"Run!" Ran Jie-shu yelled to me.

He and I ran as fast as we could to the exit. Ran Jie-shu knew the tomb like the back of his hand, and soon we were outside in the daylight.

Ran Jie-shu rolled a boulder over the secret entrance, sealing in the thieves.

"They can steal all they want now," he said. "But they won't be able to find their way out."

CHAPTER SIX

I had one thing left to do. "I am going to find the emperor," I announced. "I must tell him once again not to take mercury."

"He will kill you," Ran Jie-shu warned, but he did not leave my side. He walked with me toward the palace.

Along the way, we met a group of people walking away from the palace. Some were howling with grief. Others looked happy.

"What has happened?" I asked.

"The emperor is dead!" they told us.

Ran Jie-shu and I looked at each other. "We are too late," Ran Jie-shu said. "Let's go home."

"I have no home," I said.

He looked at me and said slowly, "You are a brave young warrior. Come live with my family and me. I would be proud to give you a home."

As we walked, I asked Ran Jie-shu
about my father's statue.

"I sculpted it from memory," he said.
"I knew in my heart that he had died.
But you are as fine a warrior as he was."

"How did you get my father's spear?"
I asked.

Ran Jie-shu smiled. "I can't tell you all
of my secrets," he said.

I was sad as we walked toward
Ran Jie-shu's house. I didn't feel much
like a warrior. The emperor was dead. I
had almost gotten us killed by trying to
stop the thieves.

Ran Jie-shu saw my downcast face. "You risked your life to save the emperor," he said. "You risked your life to protect his tomb. A warrior does not have to fight in a war to be brave."

I thought of my warrior statue in the tomb, guarding the emperor alongside my father. It was where the statue belonged.

"Besides, there is plenty of time to be brave," Ran Jie-shu said, "and only a little time to be a child."

He was right. I was welcomed into Ran Jie-shu's family. I had new brothers and sisters to play with. I forgot about being brave. I forgot about becoming a warrior.

But as I grew older, I remembered. I remembered that I was the only girl warrior in the emperor's tomb. I was The Terracotta Girl.

AFTERWORD

The First Emperor of China, Qin Shi Huangdi, was a powerful man. He was the leader of the Qin Dynasty. In 221 B.C., his soldiers defeated their enemies. Qin Shi Huangdi united the surrounding kingdoms under his rule. The Chinese empire was formed.

Emperor Qin forced his subjects to work for him. He used slave labor to build the Great Wall of China. The Great Wall was built to keep enemies from invading the empire. Many men lost their lives while building the Great Wall. The wall was so long, it took centuries to finish. Today, it is about 4,000 miles (6,400 km) long. It remains the longest structure in the world.

Emperor Qin Shi Huangdi also used slave labor to build his magnificent tomb. Emperor Qin believed that he would remain a powerful man in the afterworld. His tomb was important to him. More than 700,000 laborers helped build the tomb during a period of 38 years. It was a maze of rooms and large halls. Pearls and jewels on the ceiling represented stars. A river of mercury represented bodies of water. The terracotta army was built to protect the leader in the next world.

The emperor employed skilled craftsmen to sculpt the terracotta army. The army was complete with thousands of soldiers, horses, and chariots. The soldiers were lined up in rows. Each soldier was sculpted with different facial features. Their clothes and bodies were painted, and they held real weapons. This made each of them look extremely life-like.

The differences in each of the soldier's faces indicate that the statues were likely based on real people.

Although the tomb's riches were supposed to be secret, the tomb was raided five years after Emperor Qin Shi Huangdi's death. Weapons were stolen from the terracotta warriors, and jewels were stolen from the ceiling. The tomb was forgotten until 1974, when two farmers dug up parts of the terracotta army. Today, some of the terracotta soldiers remain intact. They are on display in various museums around the world.

GREAT WALL

Chang'an

QIN DYNASTY
in 210 B.C.

ON THE WEB

FactHound offers a safe, fun way to find Web sites related to topics in this book. All of the sites on FactHound have been researched by our staff.

1. Visit *www.facthound.com*
2. Type in this special code: 1404847375
3. Click on the FETCH IT button.

Your trusty FactHound will fetch the best sites for you!

LOOK FOR MORE *READ-IT!* READER CHAPTER BOOKS: HISTORICAL TALES: